Tagged

Eric Walters

orca soundings

ORCA BOOK PUBLISHERS

Library and Archives Canada Cataloguing in Publication

Walters, Eric, 1957-
Tagged / Eric Walters.
(Orca soundings)

Issued also in electronic formats.
ISBN 978-1-4598-0168-4 (bound).--ISBN 978-1-4598-0167-7 (pbk.)

I. Title. II. Series: Orca soundings
PS8595.A598T33 2013 jc813'.54 C2012-907467-5

First published in the United States, 2013
Library of Congress Control Number: 2012952949

Summary: A graffiti artist—the Wiz—takes on the city and the mayor in a fight to save the heart of the community.

Orca Book Publishers is dedicated to preserving the environment and has printed this book on Forest Stewardship Council® certified paper.

Orca Book Publishers gratefully acknowledges the support for its publishing programs provided by the following agencies: the Government of Canada through the Canada Book Fund and the Canada Council for the Arts, and the Province of British Columbia through the BC Arts Council and the Book Publishing Tax Credit.

Cover photography by Karlis Dravins

ORCA BOOK PUBLISHERS
PO Box 5626, Stn. B
Victoria, BC Canada
V8R 6S4

ORCA BOOK PUBLISHERS
PO Box 468
Custer, WA USA
98240-0468

www.orcabook.com
Printed and bound in Canada.

16 15 14 13 • 4 3 2 1

I'd like to thank Deadboy—
a true artist, a deep thinker
and a real gentleman.

Chapter One

"Watch your head," I said as I pulled the wire up to enlarge the hole in the fence.

Julia slipped through the opening. "You always bring us to the loveliest places."

"It will be lovely."

"You've seen it, Ian?" Oswald asked as he followed behind us.

"No, but they're always good, so I don't know why this one wouldn't be."

We slid down the concrete slope of the little waterway. At one point it had been a real river with mud banks and plants and fish, and it would have twisted and turned. Now it was as straight as an arrow, trapped between two concrete banks, with no life, more like a sewer than a stream.

"How do you even know there's something down here?" Julia asked.

"It came to my Twitter feed."

She shook her head sadly. "I can't believe you spend so much time on there."

"*I* can't believe that you haven't signed up."

"I haven't got time to waste on it."

"It's not a waste. It led me here, didn't it?"

"As I said, it's a waste of time. I'm not seeing anything except nothing, so I stand by my comment," she said.

"It's under the bridge."

"That makes sense," Oswald added. "That's out of the way, hidden from the road and prying eyes."

I thought I was starting to see something. There was more and more and—

"Wow," I said.

There it was, a painted cliff with a flock of sheep at the top, two tumbling down, one at the bottom, half of it painted right to the waterline of the real river and the rest of it underwater and unseen. Two more sheep were floating downstream, just their legs showing. There was one sheep at the top with a word balloon saying, *Didn't anybody learn to swim?*

"Well, what do you think now?" I asked Julia.

"It certainly is big."

"I wasn't asking you to measure it but to appreciate it."

"Ian, at this point all I can appreciate is that it's big," she replied.

I turned to Oswald. “What’s your opinion?”

“She’s right—it is big. But in my opinion, it’s pretty good.”

“Pretty good? It’s beautiful, amazing and incredible,” I said.

“This might be the best one. It is a real piece of art,” Oswald agreed.

“And what exactly do you know about art?” Julia challenged.

“I know what I like.”

“You like lasagna, but that doesn’t make it art.”

“First off, I love lasagna, and second off, there is an art to cooking. Edible art may be my favorite kind.”

“He’s right,” I agreed. “Food can be art. There was this sculptor who only used raw meat.”

“My butcher does that,” Oswald said. “You should see the display case in his deli.”

"No, I'm serious. It was at some fancy museum in London. He made these sculptures out of meat, and then the meat rotted over the next month, and people watched the changing sculptures."

"That is seriously disgusting!" Julia protested.

I laughed. "I imagine it didn't smell so good. Lots of people protested against it."

"I would have protested that too," Oswald added.

"You would have?" Julia asked.

"Sure, that was a waste of good food that could have been eaten."

"Typical Oswald, thinking with your stomach."

"Typical Julia, feeling with your head."

It was rare now for the tension between them to rise to the surface like this, but it still did. Friends who had become boyfriend and girlfriend trying to become just friends again—it didn't necessarily work so well. I kept that in mind whenever I thought that maybe Julia and I could be more than friends. It wasn't worth the risk.

"Beauty and art are in the eye of the beholder," I said, breaking the silence. "And according to this beholder, this was produced by an artist."

"Do you think it's the same person doing all of these?" she asked.

"Obviously," Oswald said.

"Maybe it is to you, the art *expert*, but not to us common folk," Julia said.

"Even if you can't tell by the style, you can certainly tell by the tag," I said.

I walked over and stood at the bottom right-hand corner of the creation. There was the big, stylized WIZ, written inside the outline of a sheep.

"So he thinks he's a wizard," Julia said sarcastically.

"He?" Oswald asked. "How do you know it's a guy doing this?"

"Isn't that obvious?"

"Not to me," I said before Oswald could. It probably was a guy, but I still wanted to know why she thought so.

"It's simple. Males, whether they're dogs or humans, all want to mark their territory. One will raise up his back leg, and the other, the arm holding the can of spray paint."

"So, let me get this straight. To you this is the human equivalent of a dog relieving itself on a post?" I questioned.

"More or less—and it even explains his tag name. Basically, he's taking a *Wiz* on the wall."

Oswald laughed. "Now *that* was creative. Here, take a picture of me with it."

He handed me his phone and ran over to stand in the middle of the mural.

"It's hard to get you and it in the same frame," I said.

"Go over to the other side of the creek. Use the rocks to get over," he commanded.

There was a series of rocks littering the little stream. If I jumped from one to the other, it looked like it might be possible to get across. Maybe. I hesitated.

"You can do it," Oswald said. "But Ian, be careful. I wouldn't want you to fall in—at least, not while you're holding my phone. Hurry up."

I was going to do it, but I wasn't going to hurry. I moved carefully, jumping from rock to rock until I reached the other cement bank.

"Say cheese," I said as I aimed the camera.

He smiled and held out his hands, gesturing to the painting like he was a supermodel selling perfume.

"Got it."

"Now take one of me right down here by the tag. Use the zoom to get me and it."

I fiddled around until I had him and the tag in the screen. "Nice zoom on the camera phone," I said. "Got it again."

"Thanks. This piece is fantastic, if I do say so myself."

"You're acting like you're the one who painted it," Julia scolded.

"Of course I didn't, but that doesn't mean I don't want to have my picture taken with it," he protested. "Did you design or build the Eiffel Tower?"

"Don't be ridiculous."

"Then why is there a picture in your room of you and the tower?" he asked.

"I was in Paris, and it's famous."

"When it was first put up, it was part of an advertisement for the World's Fair in Paris, and there were demands from Parisians that it be torn down because it was considered an eyesore," Oswald said.

"Yeah, right."

"He's right," I said. "Mrs. Johnson told us all about it in art class."

"Fine," she said. "But it did go on to become an icon. I'll agree that this is art if millions of people come to see it and have their pictures taken with it over the next hundred years."

"That won't happen. I doubt it will be here in a hundred hours."

"Why, will it wash off in the next rain?"

"It's permanent paint, but only permanent until the City sends a crew to paint over it," I explained.

"I heard the one with the dogs is gone already," Oswald added.

"The doggies are gone?" Julia asked. She sounded genuinely disappointed.

"*That* one you thought was art?" I asked.

She shrugged. "I just like dogs. It was cute."

"And sheep aren't cute?" Oswald asked. "I personally love sheep...as part of a balanced meal."

"Always with the stomach," she said.

"Aside from the quality of the art, I can't help wondering how he did this painting," I said.

"Seems pretty straightforward to me," Oswald said. "A ladder and a couple of long planks from one side of the creek to the other, that's all." He paused. "Well, at least that's what I was thinking...I don't know...that might work, or maybe it wouldn't."

"No, that could work," I agreed.

"It's just strange when art involves a ladder," said Julia.

"Lots of famous artists used ladders," Oswald said.

"Name one," Julia demanded.

"Rembrandt."

"What makes you think he used a ladder?" she questioned.

"Everybody knows about that. He used a ladder and some scaffolding. How do you think he painted the ceiling of that church in Italy?"

"Church...wait, do you mean the Sistine Chapel at the Vatican?"

"No, I'm pretty sure it's Italy," Oswald said. He turned slightly and winked at me. He was trying to get Julia going.

"The Vatican *is* in Italy, and it wasn't Rembrandt, it was Michelangelo!"

"Are you sure? I'm pretty sure that Angelo guy is a character in *Donkey Kong*. Isn't he Mario's brother?"

"No, that's Luigi," I said.

"Okay, then this Angelo guy was an inventor, right? Didn't he invent spaghetti and submarines or submarine sandwiches?"

"That was Da Vinci, Leonardo Da Vinci. He invented the submarine.

He was a painter, sculptor and a genius!" said Julia.

"Not to mention my favorite Ninja turtle," Oswald said.

Julia was so frustrated, she looked like she was going to explode. Oswald loved bothering Julia. He'd spent so much time playing the fool that he had it down to perfection. I worked hard not to laugh.

"So I guess I'm right. Some artists did use ladders," he said.

"But not Rembrandt," she said, looking for some satisfaction in the argument.

"Not necessarily," I said. "Some of his paintings are over ten feet tall, so he had to be standing on something."

"Come to think of it," Oswald said, "I read something about him being remarkably tall. I think he was *huge*, so maybe he didn't need a ladder."

"Rembrandt was huge?" Julia asked.

"Of course. The book said that he was a *giant* in art. To be called a giant you have to be pretty big, so he could have been seven or even eight feet tall."

"That meant that he was—" Julia stopped. She suddenly realized that Oswald was just making fun of her.

"I wonder what the Wiz was trying to say with this piece," I said, changing the subject to stop the argument.

"Probably something pretentious, like that humans are sheep," Julia said.

"Or maybe he was stressing the importance of sheep learning to swim," Oswald said.

"Maybe he just likes sheep," I added.

"Or really doesn't like sheep. After all, he is drowning them," Oswald replied.

"Or he's telling us that sheep don't float well."

"Or only float upside down and—"

"Can we just go now?" Julia asked, cutting Oswald off.

"It's probably best that we *do* go," I said. "We really shouldn't be down here. This is trespassing."

At that moment we heard voices and turned around to see half a dozen kids about our age sliding down the concrete embankment.

"It's over here!" Oswald called out.

They smiled and came in our direction.

Oswald turned to Julia. "Not millions of people, but nine is a start. Look out, Eiffel Tower."

Chapter Two

"Ian, can you hurry up and finish eating?" Oswald said to me. "I don't want to be late for class."

"Relax, we have plenty of time," I replied. "Lunch isn't over for another fifteen minutes."

"Besides, when did you start getting all worried about being late for class?" Julia asked.

"Are you questioning my dedication as a student?"

"More remembering that you were late for biology twice last week," she said.

"It's the first period. It's hard to get up that early. Besides, whose bright idea was it to move the start of school from eight forty-five to eight?"

"Probably Mr. Roberts," I said.

Our principal is a former Marine, and the Marines were into getting up early—that and being as tough as nails.

"Either way, the two of *us* seem to manage to get there on time," Julia pointed out.

Biology was the only class the three of us shared this semester.

"I guess I just need my beauty sleep more than you two," he said.

"Which would explain why you fell asleep in biology when you did get there yesterday," she said.

"No way! I was sleeping?" He turned to me. "Ian?"

"You were even snoring," I confirmed.

"Was Mr. Singh mad?"

"Not really. He said something about you finally making a contribution to class discussion. He even made you part of the lesson. He explained the role of sleep as a biological function," I said.

"I'm surprised more people don't display that biological function in his class. Mr. Singh is a great guy, but that is one boring class. Not like art appreciation. Who would have thought the class would be *that* great?"

I raised my hand. It was my suggestion—one that Oswald had agreed to and Julia hadn't. Instead, she took advanced calculus.

"Jules, you should come to class with us today," Oswald suggested.

"I have a class. Calculus."

"So miss a class. What's the worst that could happen? You only get a 95 instead of a 96?"

"Every mark counts."

"Right, that's the one that's going to stop you from getting into a good university. Come with us—Mrs. Johnson won't mind an extra student. Besides, don't you want to see the class that changed my life?" Oswald asked.

"Changed your life?" she repeated. "I think we've all been hoping for that for quite a while."

"I'm serious. Because of that class I'm giving real consideration to applying to art college next year."

"You?" both of us asked in unison.

"I don't understand the surprise. I'm very artistic," he explained.

"Again—*you*?" Julia asked.

"Sure, you've both seen samples of my work."

"When?" Julia asked.

"Where?" I asked.

"My notebook. You know I always draw all over my books."

"That's doodling! Just because you can write your name in 3-D and draw cartoon animals doesn't qualify you to go to art college."

"That's why I'm working on my portfolio," he said.

"Portfolio?" Julia questioned.

"A portfolio is a collection of an artist's work that is representative of the range of his talent and skills, offering samples and complete—"

"I know what a portfolio is," Julia said, cutting him off. "I just didn't know you were working on one or even knew what it was."

"Well, I didn't until I starting working on one. It's hard work. That's what I've been so occupied with lately."

I knew he'd been too busy to hang out a couple of times, but I'd just figured he was playing video games or watching bad movies and didn't want to be disturbed.

"It's coming along pretty well," Oswald said.

Julia got up. "Let's get going. I really *do* have to go to this art class."

"I'm so happy to have you sit in on our class, Julia," Mrs. Johnson said, "although since you're only a visitor, I'm going to ask you not to take part in our discussions."

"Of course. I understand," Julia agreed.

Oswald and I exchanged a look. We were both thinking the same thing—could Julia keep her opinions to herself for a whole period?

"A lunch," Oswald said to me out of the side of his mouth so that Julia, sitting a few seats over, couldn't hear. "The first one to say something that makes her talk gets lunch bought by the other."

"Deal. You bring your wallet and I'll bring my appetite."

"All right, let's get started," Mrs. Johnson announced.

People settled into their seats.

"Last week we were discussing how art may take many forms," Mrs. Johnson began. "That it is not simply painting or sculpture but includes poetry, plays, music, dance and more."

"Which means comic books, movies, TV, novels, hip-hop, commercials, music videos and video games," Oswald said proudly.

His first attempt to get to Julia. She didn't blink.

"All of those and more," Mrs. Johnson agreed. "Although some might argue about a few of those forms being art."

Judging from Julia's expression, I figured she was one of them.

"This week we'll focus on the way that artists not only shape their society but are shaped by it." Mrs. Johnson paused. "Let me explain. Raise your hand if you like techno-pop dance music."

A few girls raised their hands. I had to stop myself from gagging.

"In order to have techno-pop, you first need to have techno. Without the electronics, it wouldn't be possible. How many people like it when a musician releases an acoustic CD?"

Almost all hands went up, including mine.

"Then you would have loved music prior to 1900, when all music was acoustic.

Not to mention it was live, since there were no recording or broadcasting techniques. No CDs, tapes, videos, MTV or satellite radio."

"But aren't you just talking about the tools of a culture rather than the entire culture?" I asked.

"In part. There's also no doubt in my mind that if Beethoven were alive today, he'd be playing either electronic keyboards or synthesizer. But what would Shakespeare be writing?" she asked.

"Plays," Julia said, so quietly I could hardly hear her though I was sitting right beside her.

"He certainly wouldn't be writing plays," Mrs. Johnson said. Julia didn't react.

I couldn't help but wonder, if it was Mrs. Johnson who got her going, should Oswald and I buy her lunch?

"He'd probably be writing for TV or movies," somebody at the back chipped in.

"The contemporary version of playwright would be screenwriter," Mrs. Johnson said.

"So if Shakespeare was writing today, then *Romeo and Juliet* would have been a date movie," Oswald said.

"And *The Two Gentlemen of Verona* would be a buddy movie," I added.

Julia made a slight huffing sound, but no words came out.

"*Hamlet* would definitely be a horror movie," Oswald said.

"With major special-effects potential. Maybe a car chase," I said.

"Enough about Shakespeare," Mrs. Johnson said. "Others?"

"What about Jane Austen?" Oswald asked. He knew Jane was Julia's favorite writer.

"I don't know her," another student piped up. "Is she a writer?"

Julia made another little sound but didn't speak. Good—I didn't want to buy anybody else lunch.

"She wrote sweeping epic novels involving tragic relationships and romance," I explained.

"That is so easy," Oswald said. "If Jane Austen was alive today, she'd be writing Harlequin romance novels."

I almost burst into laughter but stopped myself. I turned slightly to look at Julia. I think she was biting her bottom lip to stay quiet.

"Potentially *very good* Harlequin romances," Mrs. Johnson said. "She was a wonderful writer."

I think Mrs. Johnson's comments were the only thing that saved Julia from exploding or imploding.

"Maybe she would have teamed up with that Willy Shakespeare

guy to write chick flicks," Oswald suggested.

He was on a roll. If I didn't come up with something, I'd lose this bet for sure.

"What about a famous poet like Walt Whitman?" I asked. Walt was one of Julia's favorite poets.

"Yeah, we don't really listen to poets much anymore," a girl said.

"Actually, you listen to them all the time, but, reflecting our culture, they now write lyrics," Mrs. Johnson said.

I laughed because I saw my opening. "So if Walt Whitman was alive today, he'd be a rapper. I see him throwing down some beats. I can even think of a couple of rapper names for him."

"You can?" Mrs. Johnson asked.

"Sure. Either he'd be W Squared"—kids laughed—"or, because he wrote so much about snow and ice, he could be known as The Iceman."

There was laughter and a round of applause. Julia didn't cheer, but she didn't talk. She'd been shaken, but she hadn't broken.

The bell rang to end class. The period had just zipped by.

"Well, what did you think?" I asked Julia as we walked out.

"Interesting class, but it confirmed two things that I already knew."

"What things?" Oswald asked.

"That you two are *such* idiots."

"I'm surprised you needed further confirmation of that," Oswald said. "I thought that was already a proven fact. Sort of like gravity or—"

"Did you really think you could get me to react to those cracks about Jane Austen and Walt Whitman?"

"Cracks?" I asked, trying to sound innocent. "We were simply trying to make the class more relevant for you."

"Was there a bet involved?" she asked.

"Lunch," I admitted. "Loser was supposed to buy lunch."

"In that case, since I'm obviously the winner and you two are even more obviously losers, I should get two lunches. Do either of you have any objections?"

We both shook our heads in agreement. Fair was fair.

Chapter Three

I could hear Oswald before I could see him. His car needed some work on the exhaust system, but he was trying to avoid doing it—"I don't want the muffler to be worth more than the rest of the car" was how he'd put it.

Then the car came around the corner and into view, rumbled up and stopped, brakes squealing. Oswald popped open the door from the inside—it didn't open from the outside.

"Good morning," he sang out.

"Good morning to you too. It's rare to see you up this early on a weekend."

"Weekends are the only times I can sleep to my full potential. You know me, always trying to be the best that I can be."

"So where are we off to?"

"To pick up Julia and then to the art gallery."

"No, really."

"Don't you want to pick up Julia?" he asked.

"Of course I do, but where are we really going after that?"

"We are going to the City Center Art Gallery. Seriously."

"This new you is a little hard to predict," I admitted.

"Not really. When you think of me, just think of culture, the arts and perhaps fashion."

"Fashion? Did you look in a mirror this morning?"

Oswald was wearing trackpants, no socks, lime-green Crocs, a black hoodie and a safari hat.

"Don't you think this makes a statement?" he asked.

"And just what statement were you going for?"

"The 'I'm above fashion' fashion statement."

"I'm not sure about being above fashion, but you're certainly apart from it."

"What it really means is that my mom skipped a week of laundry and these are the closest things I have to clean."

"That I not only understand but appreciate."

Julia was waiting in front of her house. She was always on time, and I knew we were a little bit late. She looked at her watch as we drove up—

her not-so-subtle way of letting us know we'd kept her waiting. I opened the door and scrunched against the dashboard so she could push my seat forward and squeeze into the backseat. I slammed the door and we started off.

"We're going to the art gallery," I announced.

"Yeah, right. Where are we really going?"

"We are," Oswald said. "We'll take in a little culture and then buy you one of your two free lunches. I just don't know why everybody is questioning my choice of activities. How can I become an artist if I don't go to see art?"

"Does the new Oswald know that the art gallery may not be open this early?" Julia asked.

"It's open."

"Are you sure? It's had its hours reduced as part of Mayor Dumfrey's cost-saving program," Julia said.

The art gallery, libraries, community theater, parks and rec programs, bus routes and pools had all had their hours or services cut to save money.

"Are you questioning my knowledge of the art world?" Oswald asked.

"That goes without saying," said Julia

"Weekdays, with the exception of Monday and Tuesday, when it's closed, it is open from ten until seven. Saturday, it is open from eleven-thirty until six, and Sunday from three until six."

"Obviously, somebody called and asked," I said.

"Or perhaps I just know intuitively. Art is my life...remember?"

"Right, and when was the last time you were even at the art gallery?" Julia asked.

"I can guarantee I was there much more recently than you," he said. She didn't respond. "But of course you have been to a couple of outdoor art showings," he added.

"That's not art—it's just fancy graffiti," she said.

"At least she's admitting that it's fancy," I said.

"Fancy or not, it's still graffiti."

"I guess that makes you and Mayor Dumfrey the same," I said.

I'd read enough in the papers to know how much he was campaigning against the city being "defaced."

"There can't be two people who are more different than him and me," she protested.

"I guess we'll have a better chance to compare the two of you next week when he comes to speak at the school," I said.

"A sure sign that the election is coming up," Julia said. "I'm already tired of his commercials—law and order, budget cuts, encouraging business, cutting taxes. So far, the only things he's cut are things I need."

"But it does sound like you support his program to paint over graffiti," Oswald said.

"Well, I guess I do. Don't you get tired of seeing people spray-painting their names and initials and symbols all over?"

"A little," I admitted. "But there's a difference between scrawling your initials on a wall and genuine art on that same wall."

"It's all still illegal."

"But one takes real skill."

"So if I rob a bank in a really skilled way, then it shouldn't be a crime?" she asked.

"Of course it's still a crime, but this is different. It's public property," I argued.

"Transit buses are public property, but that doesn't mean I'm allowed to just take one and drive it anywhere I want, does it? What about the rights of the rest of the public?" she asked.

It was obvious that she'd been giving this a lot of thought. Winning an argument with her was always difficult, and almost impossible when she'd prepared.

"Then what about that billboard up there?" Oswald asked, pointing to a massive sign.

"What about it?" she asked.

"Doesn't that infringe on my rights?"

"How?" she demanded.

"Shouldn't I have the right not to be attacked by the product that they're trying to sell? They shouldn't be able to inflict their product on me as I drive along a public road," Oswald explained.

Obviously, she wasn't the only one who had been thinking about this.

"That's different," she said. "They paid for that sign. It's not even on public property."

"But I am. Even worse, they are sending that stupid message through public property, into my eyes, and trespassing on my brain. Public space belongs to everybody, not just those who have money."

"Again, very different. If you rent a space, you can put up your message," she said.

"Any message?" he asked. "Could I rent it and put up racist comments, or pornography or—"

"Of course not!" she protested.

"So even you admit there are limits to what can go up on a billboard, even if it's paid for."

"Of course I do. Just like there are limits to what should be painted on a wall with spray paint."

It *was* hard to win an argument with her.

We pulled up to the parking lot beside the gallery.

"We really are going to the art gallery," Julia said.

"That's what I told you."

"Good. I don't care what either of you say—my definition of art doesn't include graffiti on the side of a building or on a sewer pipe."

"Let's not argue," Oswald said. "Let's just enjoy the art on the walls of the gallery."

He gave me a little look—one that Julia hadn't picked up on. He was up to something.

Chapter Four

There was no lineup for tickets and not many people inside the gallery either. Maybe cutting the morning hours of operation hadn't been that big a deal, since nobody was here even now.

"Some of my favorites in the entire collection are in this wing," Oswald said as he led us down a hallway.

"Obviously, you've been here recently if you have favorites," I said. "Impressive."

"I'm just impressed he used words like *wing* and *collection*," Julia said, shaking her head. "Other than collecting chicken wings from other people's plates, I never thought I'd hear you talking like this."

"Part of my ongoing evolution."

"How is that portfolio of yours coming along?" I asked.

"Still a lot to do, but it's developing."

"And when do we get to see it?" Julia asked.

"I'll release it slowly. I wouldn't want to overwhelm you. It all takes time. I can't just draw something. I have to wait for the muse to whisper in my ear and inspire me."

Both Julia and I started to laugh and then stopped. He was serious.

I didn't know anything about a muse, but I did know that he was working on something. We'd seen less of him over the past three weeks than ever before. I missed having him around, but really, it was almost like preparing for next year. High school was ending, and most likely the three of us were heading in different directions. I didn't even want to think about that.

The hallway was lined with paintings and sculptures. We had been moving from painting to painting as we talked. Some were very good. Some were, well...less good. Some were just plain bad. I didn't mind bad if there was at least some skill involved. There was no question that the stuff done by the Wiz was better than at least half of the things in here. Was that Oswald's plan? To show Julia that just because it was hanging in a gallery didn't mean it was good?

"One of my two favorites is on this wall," Oswald said. "See if you can pick it out."

There were five paintings. Two very large abstracts, a still-life drawing of a cityscape, a photograph of the northern lights and a little picture of...was that sheep playing poker? I was stunned. I stared at it. I recognized those sheep—five sheep playing cards, made to resemble that famous dogs-playing-poker poster.

"I see you've picked it out," Oswald said to me. "Have you read the inscription?"

I bent down to study the little name-plate beneath it. It read *Five of a kind, wool on sheepskin, created in the twisted mind of the Wiz, posted May 10 to demonstrate that nobody notices much.*

Oswald turned to Julia. "So does that make it art now that it's hanging in a gallery?"

She was, shockingly, speechless. Almost. "I'm just surprised...it's all right...I'm just confused that it's here."

"Not as confused as the board members of the art gallery will be when they finally discover it," he said.

"You mean they don't know about it?" I asked.

"Of course not. It's guerilla art. He just put it here, and nobody has noticed. It's been almost two weeks."

I laughed. "How did *you* know about this?"

"You're not the only one connected to social media," he said. "I'm surprised you didn't get a tweet about it. He has one other exhibit in the gallery. Come on and I'll show you. It's even better."

"You've seen it?"

"I told you guys I'd been here recently, it's just that neither of you believed me."

He led us out of the hallway and into the main display area. There were now other people in the gallery examining the paintings and pieces.

"There it is. The big one—the one on the far left."

"Do you mean the painting of the fire hose?" Julia asked.

"That's the one. I love realism."

"I was expecting sheep," I said.

"I think the Wiz's artistic tastes run beyond livestock."

We walked across the room toward the painting.

"I have to admit," Julia said, "it *is* very realistic-looking."

"She's right. There's a three-dimensional quality to it," I said.

Oswald reached over and opened up the "painting." It was a fire hose! Around it was a wooden frame to make it look like a gallery display.

"Read the tag," Oswald said smugly.

If you frame it, people will admire it. Next time, I frame the urinal. Wiz.

Oswald closed the door on the piece of art.

"So I guess we have no arguments. It's on the walls of a gallery, so it must be art."

Julia didn't look convinced. Or happy.

Chapter Five

We stood on a busy street in front of the newest work by the Wiz. It was a big sheep lying in a big bed, trying to get to sleep by counting people, who were drifting overhead. Two other sheep were off to the side, one saying to the other, "Even if he does get to sleep, he'll only have nightmares about mutton."

"I'm not particularly impressed," Julia said.

"Shocking, you not being impressed," I said. "Would you be more impressed if it was hanging *on* a wall instead of painted *onto* a wall?"

"It's just not that good."

"I think it's *very* good," I said.

Oswald yawned loudly.

"Look, even Oswald the great artist finds it boring," she said.

"He's just tired. Probably up late working on his portfolio."

"I was working late on it," he said, "but I think Julia's right. As I'm standing here looking up at it, I don't think it's as good as the others. Just too derivative."

"Wow," I said. "Is that, like, your word for the day?"

"Oswald is right. It's like he wants to keep the same theme of sheep but without any new, really good ideas. A sheep counting humans to get to sleep is not creative or original," Julia explained.

"Do you think it's easy to come up with new ideas all of the time, to hit it out of the ballpark every time up to bat?" Oswald asked.

We both stared at him. He seemed to be taking this way too personally.

"Sorry. I didn't mean to insult your favorite artist," Julia said.

"I guess I just know how hard it is...artist to artist." He handed me his phone. "Anyways, I'd still like a picture of it. Somebody needs to record it before it's gone."

"I heard the swimming sheep are gone," I said.

"Why didn't they leave that one alone?" Julia protested.

"Sounds like you started to appreciate it."

"I didn't *not* like it. Besides, it wasn't like it was hurting anybody there, under the bridge. Why didn't they take the money it cost to remove it and apply it to longer hours at the library?"

"Or the art gallery. I wonder if his two things are still on display?" I asked.

"The sheep playing poker is gone," Oswald said.

"So somebody finally discovered it was a fraud," Julia said.

"Nope. Finally the glue holding it on the wall failed, and it fell to the floor," Oswald explained. "I heard the fire hose is still drawing rave reviews."

"This one here isn't going to last very long," Julia said. "It's too busy, with too much traffic passing by during the day."

She was right. There was a steady stream of cars and pedestrians, not to mention the hundreds of apartment windows that overlooked it.

"It's a lot quieter at night," Oswald said. "Well, it must be, and of course darker, right?"

"Darker, but not dark. There are a lot of streetlights," I said.

"But part of Mayor Dumfrey's cost-savings program is that he's not replacing burned-out streetlights as often, so maybe it isn't that light," Julia said.

"Still, even at night, even with some lights out, even with not many people being on the street, it still would have taken hours to paint."

Oswald shook his head. "Not hours. He's using a couple of stencils, so it would be fairly fast."

"Stencils?" Julia asked.

"Big cardboard or paper cutouts. See how the two sheep at the bottom are identical, and the flying humans are based on two basic shapes," Oswald explained.

"You're right," Julia agreed. "I hadn't noticed."

Oswald pointed at himself. "I have the eye of an artist."

"I'm not prepared to admit that until I've seen a few pieces from your portfolio," Julia said.

"All shall unfold as it should," he said. "Now, can you please take my picture?"

He walked over to the big painting, and I framed it so that he and the whole painting would be in the shot.

"What do you think would happen if he was caught doing this?" Julia asked.

"He'd definitely be arrested for vandalism," I said. "The only question is, would he get a fine, have to pay for the expense of cleaning the walls, or go to jail?"

"Do you really think jail would be a possibility?" Julia asked.

"If our mayor has anything to do with it, he'd want him jailed for a very long time."

"Let's just hope he's smart enough not to get caught," Julia said.

“And more important, smart enough to come up with some new ideas,” Oswald added.

Chapter Six

Einstein was correct—time is relative. It had only been about sixty minutes that we'd been sitting here in the auditorium, listening to the mayor speak, but it seemed more like six hundred minutes. Squeezed into the auditorium with every kid in the school, I felt like the oxygen in the room had all been consumed and the only source left was the hot air streaming out of the mouth of the mayor—what a delightful image.

On stage with the mayor, in two rows of seats, were our teachers and our principal, Mr. Roberts. Watching them squirm and fight to stay awake was my only source of entertainment. And, of course, being in the very front row of the auditorium—the location where Julia as student president insisted on sitting—gave us a great seat for watching but a terrible place for hiding.

The mayor was directly in front of us, so close that I could see the sweat on his brow. He did sweat a lot. Directly behind him were his bodyguards. They were two huge men dressed in almost identical black suits and wearing identical dark sunglasses. Those sunglasses would sure come in handy—nobody could see if your eyes were closed during the speech. I'd heard that the bodyguards went everywhere with him.

Was he expecting an attack from some librarian angry about the shorter hours, or thinking a patron of the art gallery would spray him with a paint gun?

I forced myself to stay awake and focus on what he was saying.

"As mayor, I have worked tirelessly to let people know that this city is open for business," he said.

Unless you were a library, art gallery or swimming pool, of course, and then you were open less often because of him.

"Potholes have been fixed, red tape has been cut and the gravy train at City Hall has been derailed!"

I couldn't help but picture a train off the rails, gravy running through the streets. I wondered if the Wiz had a hotline where I could make suggestions for his next piece.

"Businesspeople who come to this city need to know that this is a place where businesses and private property are respected. We must fight against those who threaten the public good."

I had an image of him dressed as a superhero in a little spandex outfit with a cape—that was one bad image.

"They are all criminals, whether they wield a gun or a knife or a spray can and whether they rob a bank or deface our public buildings and spaces."

What an idiot. He was now equating a gun with a spray can.

"And while catching criminals should be left to the police, I have made a personal commitment to remove or paint over any graffiti within twenty-four hours of its being discovered."

I was more than willing to bet that his commitment didn't involve him personally doing any of the actual work, with or without the superhero costume.

I looked over at Oswald. He was awake and listening, actually on the edge of his seat. Obviously, the mayor had gotten his attention.

"We are involved in an epic battle to reclaim our city!" the mayor yelled, hitting his hand against the podium.

"Wow, an epic battle," Oswald repeated, loud enough for a number of students to turn in his direction.

"And as mayor, I am the commander in chief of that battle!"

"You're the man!" Oswald yelled out.

The mayor started slightly in reaction, pausing for a split second before he started up again. Mr. Roberts glared in our direction, and I wanted a place to hide or a few seats' separation from Oswald.

"In conclusion," he said—now he'd gotten my attention—"it is important that we all work hard to leave our mark on the world. But that mark should be at school, on the playing field or ultimately in the profession that you choose, not on the side of some building. Thank you."

There was a slight pause as people waited, hoping it was actually over, then polite applause. Oswald jumped to his feet and began cheering loudly. I reached out and pulled him back down, but he kept clapping enthusiastically.

Mr. Roberts, one eye on Oswald, walked across the stage and shook the mayor's hand. They exchanged a few words and then, as the mayor sat down, Mr. Roberts came to the microphone.

"We were going to field a few questions, but I'm afraid we've run out of time. Thank you for your polite behavior. You should now proceed to your period-two classes."

There was a smattering of applause, and kids got to their feet and started to leave.

"What got into you?" Julia asked Oswald.

"I was cheering because that guy is a real inspiration."

"Him?"

"Weren't you listening at all? He drove himself to the top."

"It wasn't a very far drive," Julia said. "He's rich from his family's business."

"Gee, thanks for destroying the illusion about him being 'one of us,'" Oswald said, "but still, he's an inspiration—at least to me."

"And you're now suddenly in favor of him painting over street art?" Julia asked.

"Maybe him painting over it is simply the mayor's attempt to create his own street art," Oswald suggested. "All I know is that I leave this auditorium feeling inspired."

Chapter Seven

"The arts have a long history of political comment and protest," Mrs. Johnson began. "Jack and Jill went up the hill to fetch a pail of water. Who knows the next verse?"

"Jack fell down and broke his crown," a bunch of us chorused. "And Jill came tumbling after."

"Good," she said. "Now, who knows what that little ditty is about?"

"I'm going to go out on a limb here and suggest that it is part of a political comment or protest," Oswald said.

"It dates from the French Revolution. Jack is King Louis XVI and Jill is Marie Antoinette. They lost their crowns—their heads, which were cut off," she explained. "Humpty Dumpty is believed to refer to the despised King Richard III of England and his defeat at Bosworth Field in 1485."

"And all the king's horses and all the king's men couldn't put Humpty together again," I said. "I guess that makes sense."

"But those are just nursery rhymes," somebody said.

"Which we all know is a form of art," Mrs. Johnson replied. "Let's turn to what is unquestionably one of the most famous art pieces in history by one of our greatest artists. Michelangelo hated one of the cardinals, so he painted his face into the Sistine Chapel."

"That sounds more like a compliment than a protest," I said.

"Perhaps you need to do a little research and see where he put that face. The cardinal was furious and complained to the Pope, who replied that he should talk to God instead. Another example is Picasso's famous work *Guernica*, which he painted in response to the German bombing of Guernica during the Spanish Civil War. Can anybody come up with modern examples of art as protest or comment?"

"Political cartoons in the editorial section of newspapers," somebody mentioned.

"And the comics, like *Doonesbury*," another added.

"*The Simpsons* and *South Park* are always making fun of politicians," Oswald added.

"All great examples. By using the medium of art, the artist is given not only a platform but also some protection," Mrs. Johnson explained.

"This stuff is so amazing," Oswald said to me as an aside. "Who would have thought you could actually learn things in school?"

"I think that's sort of the idea behind the whole school concept."

"Really? Good to know. Now, would you keep it down? I'm trying to learn here."

Chapter Eight

"I'm beginning to think the mayor isn't the only person engaged in an epic battle for the walls of this city," I said as we stared up at the latest street-art piece.

"And it's a battle between a half-wit and a true wit," Julia added.

"So obviously you like it," Oswald said.

"I like it a lot."

We were looking at a new piece by the Wiz. It was as tall as a billboard, occupying the whole side of a building. There were about twenty sheep in it, and in the middle there was a big black wolf. The wolf was wearing a sheepskin and saying, "I'm just like you—I like sheep." Off to one side were two more sheep, one saying to the other, "He always drools when he says that." The face of the wolf looked a lot like the mayor's.

"That wolf really does look like Dumfrey—that same smug, self-satisfied little smile," Julia said.

"He did capture him pretty well," I agreed.

"And even the words he's saying. He said that at our school, didn't he?" Julia said.

"He said he was a sheep?" Oswald asked.

"Of course not!" Julia said. "He said that he was just like us, right?"

"I think so," I said.

"Wait...does that mean that the Wiz is a student at our school?" she asked.

"Wow, I hadn't thought of that. It *must* be."

"I guess the cat is finally out of the bag," Oswald said. "I'm sorry for keeping it from you, but I'm the Wiz."

"Yeah, right," Julia said. "And I'm really Catwoman."

"No, really I am," Oswald said.

"It's more *likely* it's me," Julia said.

"That would make perfect sense," I agreed. "All that stuff about you hating it was your cover, sort of like Bruce Wayne not speaking well of Batman."

"I bet it's one of those artsy kids, the ones nobody pays any attention to," she said.

"I can identify with that," Oswald said.

"Wait a second," I said. "It might not be somebody from our school. I bet the mayor says pretty much the same speech all the time. I can't imagine him making up a new one wherever he goes."

"You're right. I think I've read some of those same comments in the newspaper and heard little clips from him on the news saying just about the same things," she agreed.

"But it just would have been cool if the Wiz did go to our school," I said.

"Very cool," Oswald agreed. "But one thing is for sure—I think another shot has been fired in the epic battle for the walls of our cities. And speaking of shots, could you take my picture with it, please?"

Chapter Nine

I turned up the volume on the TV. I'd already caught a little of the story on the early news broadcast at 6:00—Julia had called and told me to tune it in—but I wanted to see all of it on the 11:00 news.

"In local news, our election has taken a most unexpected turn," the announcer said. "It appears that the greatest challenger to our mayor isn't even on the ballot."

The scene shifted to Mayor Dumfrey, standing in front of "his" mural along with a woman—a very attractive woman—holding a microphone. This was the interview I'd seen a little of. The cameraman had angled the shot so that you could see the mural being painted over, but the wolf in sheep's clothing hadn't been covered yet. The resemblance between the mayor and the wolf was amazing.

"Mayor Dumfrey," the interviewer began, "what are your comments on what we see going on behind us?"

"As we can all see, I'm keeping my word to battle the misguided young person or people who are defacing our city."

"You must admit that there is a certain amount of talent involved in this street art," she said.

"Please don't legitimize an act of vandalism by referring to it as *art*. This is simply vandalism. Real art is hanging in the gallery."

Obviously, he hadn't seen the fire hose in the City Center Art Gallery. Maybe if he hadn't reduced the hours the gallery was open, he would have seen it.

"This is nothing more than a criminal activity. It is an affront to the good and honest citizens of this fine city," he continued.

"And, some might say, an even bigger affront to you personally?"

"All criminal activities offend me," he said.

"I'm referring to the face on the wolf," she said. "The resemblance between you and the wolf is remarkable."

The screen switched to a two-shot—the mayor and the wolf. It *was* a great replica.

"I personally don't see it."

"And the cartoon word bubbles," she went on. "They are paraphrasing some of the words from your speeches."

"Imitation, even misguided imitation, is the most sincere form of flattery. Even in his twisted mind, this criminal still sees some wisdom in my words."

I had to give him credit for twisting things around. He might even get some votes out of this.

"I guess in some ways he's paying me a compliment without even meaning to. In the same way a criminal knows a good policeman—and our city has some of the finest in the world—he knows me. And if he's watching right now," the mayor said, looking directly into the camera, "I want him to know there's a lot more gray paint where this came from. I can paint over anything you do, so stop wasting your time and get a real job."

He was formally throwing down the gauntlet. This was not the last battle in this war.

"And for the rest of you watching, remember that a vote for me is a vote against crime. Criminals don't own this city—it belongs to *me* and you."

I couldn't help noticing that he put a lot more emphasis on the *me* than the *you*.

"Thank you, Mayor Dumfrey. This is Candy Knight reporting."

Viewers were taken back to the news desk, where the anchorman made a semifunny comment and then went on to another story. My cell phone rang. It was 50-50—Oswald or Julia. I looked at the caller ID. It was Oswald—his home phone.

"Did you see that?" I asked.

There was a pause. "See what?" It was Oswald's mother.

"The news. I was watching the news, the eleven o'clock news," I explained.

"I'm so sorry to be disturbing you by calling so late," she said.

"It's not that late."

"I was afraid I'd wake you up."

My parents were asleep, but a call to my cell phone wouldn't wake them. But why was she calling me to begin with?

"Oswald is probably long asleep," she said.

I almost said "Thanks for sharing that" but didn't.

"He's been sleeping a lot lately," she said. "Probably a growth spurt."

Or he was just being lazy. Either way, I'd noticed the same thing—he was even falling asleep in class. Early starts did not agree with him.

"Could you please do me a favor and remind him that he has a dentist appointment after school tomorrow?" she asked.

"Sure, I could do that." At least this call now made some sense...well, not much, but some. I had to admit that Oswald would probably forget his head if it wasn't loosely attached to his shoulders, so a reminder wouldn't hurt.

"It's just so nice of your family to let him sleep over at your house so often," she said.

"That's never a problem," I replied.

"I never would have imagined that the dust and paint of the renovations would bother him so much," she said. "Soon it'll be over, though, and he can start sleeping at home more instead of at your house."

I knew about the renovations. But she seemed to think he was here tonight sleeping over, and he hadn't slept here in over a month.

"Just remind him about the dentist, and again, thanks to you and your parents," she said.

"Oh, believe me, I'll tell him," I said. "Good night."

I hung up. Oswald wasn't here. His parents thought he was. I knew he wasn't. They had the luxury of thinking he was here, so they weren't worried. I didn't have that luxury—I was worried. I picked up my phone again and punched in his cell number.

Chapter Ten

"Come on, pick it up," I mumbled as the phone continued to ring and ring and ring.

What was I going to do if he didn't answer? It wasn't like I could call his parents back or wake up my parents and ask them what to do. I guessed I could call Julia and—

"Hey, Ian, why are you calling so late?"

His voice was low and quiet, as if I'd woken him up.

"I guess I just wanted to remind you that you have a dentist appointment tomorrow."

"I do?"

"Yeah, right after school. Trust me—I know."

"I believe you, but couldn't this wait until tomorrow? I was asleep."

"Really?" I exclaimed.

"Could you keep it down? I don't want to wake up my parents."

"Funny, your mother seemed pretty awake when she called me a few minutes ago."

"My mother? You've got to be wrong. She's been asleep for a while. Maybe *you* were asleep and dreaming about my mother...and that is so wrong on so many levels, I'm not even sure we can be friends anymore."

"Oswald. I want the truth. Now."

There was silence. I almost wondered if the call had been dropped or he'd hung up.

"It's sort of hard to explain, and I'm really not in a great position to have a conversation right now. How about if we talk about it tomorrow?" he suggested.

"How about you tell me now or I'm going to call and explain what I don't know to your parents?"

He laughed. "We both know you're not going to do that."

He'd called my bluff. He was right. I wouldn't do that.

"Come on, no secrets between best friends. Just tell me."

"How about if I just show you. Can you get out of the house without your parents knowing?"

"Sure. They're asleep, but I could always wake them up and tell them I'm sleeping at your house. That excuse is working *so* well for you."

"Come to the northeast corner of Erin Mills Parkway and Dundas. There's a big parking lot. I'll meet you there."

"But—"

"No buts. You want the answer, just come."

Chapter Eleven

I rode my bike along the side streets, avoiding main roads where there was still pedestrian traffic. The side streets were less traveled, and the only people I saw were in passing cars, and they ignored me on my bike with no headlight.

I'd decided not to wake my parents. I'd left a note taped to my door—*Sleeping at Oswald's*. If I got home without them knowing I'd gone out, I'd remove the sign, but if they got up and discovered me missing, they wouldn't panic or call the police.

Riding alone at night in the semi-darkness, I sort of appreciated the mayor's anti-crime stance. The only problem was, there was a good chance I was going to kill Oswald when I found him. What was he up to? I guessed I wouldn't have to wait long to find out.

I glided into the parking lot. There was no sign of Oswald or his car. Maybe he was behind the building. Slowly moving away from the street-lights and occasional car on the road, I kept going. Still there was no Oswald, no cars, no people. Just plenty of places for a criminal to hide and—

"Ian!"

I skidded to a stop. It was Oswald, but I couldn't see him.

"Where are you?"

"Here."

I could detect a general direction from the voice but still couldn't see him.

"Over where? I can't see you!"

"Not so much *over* as *up*. Look up."

I looked up. There he was, five meters above my head, standing on the edge of a gigantic billboard.

"Fancy meeting you here," he said. "What a strange coincidence."

"What are you doing up there?" I yelled.

He shushed me. "I know we *are* outside, but do you think you could use your inside voice?"

"What are you doing?" I hissed.

"Stash your bike in the bushes. There's a hole in the fence. Come up and see for yourself."

Hiding the bike did seem like a good idea. Hiding me would have been better. Being at home would have been the best idea. The billboard was behind the parking lot, poking out of a cluster of bushes and small trees. I maneuvered the bike through the hole in the fence and along a little path to a big pole where Oswald's bike was stashed. I wondered why he'd taken his bike instead of his car.

There were metal rungs on the pole, forming a ladder leading up. Down here I was hidden by the bushes. Up there I wouldn't be. Then again, I hadn't come out to hide but to find out what was going on, and the truth was at the top of the pole.

I started up the rungs. The first few steps left me hidden, the next ones got me above the bush line, and then I neared the top. Here the pole went through a hole in the ledge, which was much wider than it had looked from below. I poked my head through the hole.

"Oswald?" I called out.

"I was getting worried. You take a wrong turn on the pole or what?"

"What are you—?" I stopped mid-sentence. I already had my answer, all around and above me. Oswald was standing on a rickety little wooden ladder leaning against the billboard. He was wearing a black hoodie and black overalls—both were splattered with paint. On the ledge were cans of spray paint, and above him some painting had already been done.

"Are you crazy?" I demanded.

"Inside voice, remember?"

"Are you crazy?" I hissed.

"I think you've known me long enough to know the answer to that question."

"You can't just do something like this. It takes time and talent and—"

"Are you saying the Wiz doesn't have talent?" he asked.

"Of course he has—" Oh my goodness. "You're the Wiz."

"Oswald, Oz, the Wizard of Oz, the Wiz. I'm surprised you didn't put it together before this," he said.

I was speechless.

"Could you pass me up that stencil by your feet?"

For a split second, I not only couldn't speak but couldn't comprehend. Finally it clicked in, and I bent down and picked up an oval cardboard cutout. I passed it up to him.

"Does that look like it would make a good egg?" he asked.

"Um, sure—a really big egg."

"That's what I'm after. And could you do me one more favor? Could you take a bunch of pictures while I'm doing this? I don't have any shots of me working. They'd go great in my portfolio."

"This is what you meant by your portfolio?"

"I told you I was putting one together for my application to art school."

"But you didn't say it was these."

"I did tell you and Julia that I was the Wiz, but neither of you believed me, remember?"

"I remember. We just thought you were joking around again. I don't usually believe half of what you say."

"Fair enough. The secret is to figure out which half to believe. You guessed wrong."

He climbed farther up the ladder. In a special belt around his waist was a makeshift holster holding cans of spray paint and some brushes. Just as he was about to start, he pulled a ski mask out of his pocket and slipped it on. It had a skull on it.

"What's with the mask?" I asked.

"It hides my identity…and it's pretty darn cool, don't you think?"

It was cool. The only thing cooler was that I was about to watch the Wiz at work.

I snapped another picture. I'd taken so many, I didn't know how much more memory my phone had. I hadn't been painting, but I'd been working. I'd been up and down the ladder, taking pictures from all angles of Oswald at work. Four times I'd gone out into the parking lot to get a wider perspective on the entire painting. It was impressive, even in the dark. My only fear was that the continual flashes of my camera would give him away. I just hoped they looked like lightning to anybody watching from a distance.

"Well?" Oswald asked.

"It is nothing short of spectacular. A masterpiece."

Oswald had painted a brick wall. Sitting on the top of the wall was a large egg with the mayor's face, wearing a bib. On its bib were the words *Humpty Dumfrey*. Below it were two little eggs in matching black suits and dark sunglasses. One of them was saying, "I think the yolk may be on us." And the other replied, "I don't think we can put this together again." Off to the side were the signature sheep, one of them saying, "I love the smell of raw egg in the morning."

"I can't wait to see the whole thing in the light of day," I said.

"I'm afraid you're going to have to wait until after school unless you want to get caught. We have to get out of here before the sun comes up."

"Oh, of course. I hadn't thought about that."

Oswald pulled his mask off, stuffed it in the pocket of his hoodie and then removed both the hoodie and his overalls. They were covered in paint—

a rainbow of colors that matched those in the painting. Carefully he put them into his backpack, which already held cans of spray paint and the folded-up stencils—eggs, sheep and bricks.

"What about the ladder?"

"Too big to carry. I brought it yesterday with my car."

"Why didn't you bring the car now?" I asked.

"Cars have license plates. I couldn't risk anybody seeing my car and noting the plate."

"Smart."

"Don't sound so surprised. Besides, the ladder is just something I threw together with things the contractors working on my house tossed out. No identifying material, no way to trace it back to me, so we leave it. A souvenir for the mayor, if he wants it."

"Great, let's get—" I broke off as a car pulled off the road and into the parking lot, its headlights leading the way. We both froze.

"It's a car," I said, stating the obvious.

"No, it isn't just a car. It's a *police* car!"

Both of us dropped flat, pressing ourselves against the ledge. We were now hidden from view. Unfortunately, the billboard wasn't. All they had to do was look up and they'd see it—although it *was* dark, and the sign wasn't lit up. Maybe they wouldn't.

"They're coming this way," Oswald said.

Or maybe they *could* see us. I pressed myself even flatter on the ledge.

The police car came to a stop almost right underneath us. The headlights went off, and it got darker. And then the engine stopped.

"What do you think they're doing?" Oswald whispered.

"I think it's customary for them to turn off the engine before they make an arrest."

"Then I would assume they'd also get out of the car, unless they plan on having us fall directly onto their vehicle. I don't think they've seen us, or they'd be getting out."

"Maybe they're just taking a break," I suggested. "Like lunch hour."

"It's four in the morning, so either it's a very early or a very late lunch," Oswald said. "Either way, we need to just lay low and wait them out."

"Even if it's an hour?" I whispered.

"The sun doesn't come up for at least two, so unless you have another alternative you'd like to suggest, what choice do we have?"

"If we snuck down the pole, we could go out through the back—climb over the fence."

"They'd probably see us going down the pole—and even if they didn't, what about our bikes?"

"We could come back and get them later," I said.

"I don't think we have much of a later. Once the sun comes up, the painting will be discovered, along with the bikes," Oswald said.

"I'd prefer they find the bikes than find us."

"If they find the bikes, they *do* find us. Bikes have registration numbers. It wouldn't take Sherlock Holmes to trace them back to us."

"And then they'd know who did this, and you'd be in big trouble," I said.

"We'd *both* be in big trouble."

Strangely, I hadn't even thought of me being in trouble. I was so worried about Oswald, it had just sort of slipped my mind that I was going to get in trouble too. Denial was an incredible thing.

"So just lay back and relax," Oswald said.

"I am laying back, but relaxing isn't going to happen."

"Close your eyes. Think nice thoughts. Just use your imagination and go to your happy place."

"I can do that. I'm imagining that I'm on a tropical island...warm sun...and I'm not lying on the ledge of a big billboard with a police car right below me."

Oswald laughed and then stopped himself. He had been louder than either of us would have liked.

"Sorry," he whispered. "Especially about getting you into this. I didn't mean to get you into trouble."

"If I was you, I'd be less worried about the police and more worried about Julia. She's going to kill you when she finds out you kept all this from her."

He didn't answer right away. "You stay up here, and I'm going down to turn myself in. I'm going to ask to be taken into protective custody."

"That won't do you any good," I joked. "She'll just wait until you get out and then kill you."

I looked over the ledge. The police car was dark and silent. Were they having lunch or an extended nap?

"So what do you think of my portfolio?" Oswald asked. "Do you think it's good enough to get me into art college?"

"If I was the dean of admissions, I wouldn't let you in."

"You wouldn't? Why not?" he asked.

"I'd be afraid that the first time you failed a course, you'd paint a wall at the college with a mural featuring my face on the body of a donkey."

Oswald chuckled. "I'm not through with the mayor yet."

"How about if we save those new ideas for tomorrow? I'm going to close my eyes and transport myself to a happy place...away from you."

Chapter Twelve

I opened my eyes. Why was it so bright? Hadn't I closed the blinds? And it was chilly and—I sat bolt upright as I remembered exactly where I was. The sun was up, and there was traffic flowing on Erin Mills Parkway. A few cars were already in the parking lot below us, but the police car was gone.

"Oswald, get up!" I yelled.

He sat up. His expression was both shocked and confused.

"We have to—"

"Get away, quickly!" he screamed.

He grabbed his pack, and we went through the opening and down the pole rungs. I had to move fast to stop him from stomping on my fingers. I jumped over the last few rungs. I grabbed my bike and thumped it along the path, through the hole in the fence and into the parking lot. Oswald was right behind me.

"Ride, ride," he screamed.

He threw his pack on his back, and we raced away, hitting the sidewalk and then the road, where traffic was racing by. We didn't stop—we just picked up speed, racing along the edge of the road, a combination of fear and adrenalin pushing us forward. Oswald turned off the road and onto a path, finally stopping in a thick patch of trees.

"We're okay...I think," Oswald panted.

"Good. We got away...clean away."

"What time is it?" he asked.

"Almost seven thirty."

"Seven thirty!" he exclaimed. "School starts in less than thirty minutes, and I can't afford to be late. Mr. Singh threatened that one more late from me, and he'd demonstrate that his ceremonial kirpan could have actual uses."

"He wouldn't actually stab you," I said.

"No, but he did say that he'd use it to cut my marks in half."

"If we go right now, we can make it. Just."

"Okay, let's ride."

We rolled into the school parking lot. It was filled with cars inching along, either dropping kids off or looking for a parking spot. There was only a minute or two to spare.

"Go—leave your bike with me and I'll lock it up," I said.

He jumped off his bike.

"And you don't have time to go to your locker. Just give me your pack, and I'll put it in my locker."

"But you'll be late."

"I can afford to be late. Just go...you Wiz, you."

He smiled, handed me the pack and then raced off to class.

Chapter Thirteen

I glanced over at Oswald. He looked as tired as I felt. He had made it to class on time. I'd been a couple of minutes late, but Mr. Singh hadn't said anything. I was just surprised that neither of us had fallen asleep so far and the period was almost over. I was starting to drift off now, though, and figured I'd take a little nap in second period.

There was a knock on the door, and by the time I turned to look, Mr. Roberts had stepped into the room.

"I'm very sorry to disturb your class," he said, "but I need to speak to two students."

There are lots of students in this room. Please, please, please don't say—

"Oswald and Ian," he said.

Great. Perfect.

"It shouldn't take long," he said.

Okay, maybe it would be all right. There might be dozens of reasons why he'd want to speak to us. Besides, what we'd done last night was off school property and outside of school hours.

We both got to our feet. I flashed a weak smile. Oswald looked worried. Julia, who knew nothing about anything, still looked worried for us. We followed Mr. Roberts out into the hall, and I skidded to a stop. There were two police officers waiting for us, and even worse, the mayor and his bodyguards were just a dozen feet farther down the hall. This was bad—this was awful. Strangely, though, I couldn't help thinking that Mayor Dumfrey really did look like the egg Oswald had just painted. Or maybe the egg looked like him.

"These officers have requested to speak to you two," Mr. Roberts explained.

"Sorry to take you out of class," one of them said. "I'm sure it's nothing but a misunderstanding."

He smiled. That was supposed to be reassuring. Instead, I thought about a crocodile smiling before biting me.

He held out his hand. "But first, introductions. Which one of you is Ian?"

"That's me." I offered my hand and we shook, but then he brought my hand up and looked at it, turning it over, staring at it. What was he doing?

"It's not him," he said. "His hand is clean. No paint."

"What?"

He released my hand.

"But look here," the other officer said. He was holding Oswald's hand up in the air. There, visible for everybody to see, was red and blue paint.

"And if I'm not mistaken, those are some of the colors and shades used on the latest painting," he said.

"You mean the latest vandalism!" the mayor snorted. "Take him away and throw him in jail!"

I grabbed Oswald's other hand. "You're not taking him anywhere!"

"Sorry, Ian, you'd better stay out of this—they're police officers," Mr. Roberts said.

"Then they should know the law better than anybody. He's a minor, and they can't take him anywhere or question him without first seeking the permission of his parents or offering a lawyer to be part of the interview if parents or guardians cannot be found."

"Look who thinks he's a lawyer!" the mayor snorted. "Arrest the one for vandalism, and the other for resisting arrest!"

"Ian?" Mr. Roberts asked. "How do you know this?"

"I took law last semester. I got a 92."

Mr. Roberts turned to the officers. "Well?"

"If he isn't eighteen, then we have to—"

"I'm *not* eighteen, not for another month!" Oswald said.

"So is Ian correct?" Mr. Roberts asked.

The officer looked like he didn't want to answer. Finally he nodded his head in agreement. "He needs to have a parent or a lawyer."

"And he's going to have both!" I exclaimed.

I pulled out my phone, then suddenly remembered that it was against school policy to use it on school property or during school hours.

"This time, it is an emergency," Mr. Roberts said, reading my reaction.

"Thanks, sir." I hesitated for a second. I had two parents who were lawyers. They were both really good lawyers. But one of them scared me far more than the other. I punched in that number.

It rang and rang and—"Mom, I need your help...no, I'm okay, it's Oswald... the police are here, so I need you to come to the school...what?...sure...okay, I'll tell him. See you at school."

I hung up. "Oswald, my mother said—and I quote—that you 'are, for the first time in your life, to keep your mouth completely shut.' Understand?"

He nodded. He looked scared.

"Your mother is a lawyer?" the officer asked.

"Both my parents are lawyers."

"Wait. Your last name is Cheevers. So that means your parents are Sarah and David Cheevers."

"Great," the other officer said. "Just great."

That reaction and the looks on their faces gave me some satisfaction and a little confidence. I got the feeling they were more than a little afraid of my mother too.

"I suggest we get out of the hall. It's almost time for class change," Mr. Roberts said. "We can wait in my office."

"This is ridiculous!" the mayor bellowed.

"What part of following the law do you find most ridiculous?" Mr. Roberts asked him.

The mayor looked speechless, perhaps for the first time in his political life.

I was going to say something now that would get him talking.

"He shouldn't even be here," I said, pointing directly at the mayor. "Separation of the legal and political process is as guaranteed in our system as separation of church and state."

"Are you trying to kick me out?" he demanded. "I can be here if I want to—"

"No, you can't. This is a police investigation, and if you don't leave, then I think somebody should contact the press," I said.

The mayor looked like he was going to pull a full Humpty Dumfrey and explode into a million small pieces. I wondered if his bodyguards could put him together again.

"I'm surprised the kid only got a 92," one of the officers said to the other. "Again, he is correct about those eligible to be part of police process. I guess somebody might want to explain that to our captain."

"But...but...but..." the mayor sputtered.

"I'm not even sure why he's on school property to begin with," I added. "Shouldn't he be escorted off or charged with trespassing?"

"I'm the mayor! This is my city, and I can go anywhere I want in it!"

"No, you can't," Mr. Roberts said. "I happen to know the Education Act fairly well, and Ian is, once again, correct. But as principal, I will extend a courtesy and allow you to wait in the vice-principal's office." He turned to me. "If that is acceptable?"

"As long as he doesn't talk to Oswald or be present when he's being questioned," I said.

"You really think you can run this, don't you?" Mayor Dumfrey said, trying to stare me down. "I'm the mayor and—"

"And you shouldn't be able to talk to me or any other student, either, especially when you attempt to intimidate me like that," I said.

The mayor started toward me, and Mr. Roberts stepped in between us and stared him down. Mr. Roberts, former Marine that he was, and standing taller and wider than the officers and the bodyguards, was doing a little intimidation of his own.

"And my mother also said that I was to stay with Oswald the entire time until she arrives," I said. That was the first thing I'd said that was a lie.

"That's no problem," the officer said.

Mr. Roberts turned to the mayor. "Let me escort you to my vice-principal's office."

Mayor Dumfrey nodded, but looked over at me. "Some people think they're pretty smart," he muttered as he was led away.

One of the officers turned to the other. "I'm willing to bet *he* never got a 92 in anything."

I laughed, and the mayor, still walking away, looked back at me angrily. He must have thought I was laughing at him. He was right.

"That guy is a piece of work," the officer said under his breath. He looked at Oswald. "Couldn't you have worn gloves or used some paint thinner to clean your hands?"

Oswald went to answer.

"Not a word!" I yelled before he could speak.

"I wasn't trying to get a statement," the officer said. "I was just trying to give him some future advice. He's not the only one who's unhappy about us being here."

"Okay, sure. Can I have a minute before we go? I just need to gather up our stuff."

"We have lots of time before your mother arrives."

I looked directly at Oswald. He made a motion like he was zipping his mouth closed. I hurried into the classroom and found the entire class staring at me. I realized that not only had the door been open a little bit, but they had been listening to everything that had been said.

"Can I speak to Julia for a second, sir?" I asked Mr. Singh.

"You may take as much time as you need. I would not wish to infringe on your rights."

I pulled her into the corner.

"What is this—"

"Just listen. No questions. You have to go to my locker. In it is Oswald's backpack, and in there are some clothes and cans of spray paint."

"Spray paint!"

"Keep your voice down."

"But why is there spray paint?" she asked.

"From last night. Oswald is the Wiz."

"And neither of you told me?" she exclaimed.

"This isn't about your hurt feelings. You have to go and get it and hide it, destroy it or something."

"And if I can do that, he'll be all right?" she asked.

"I don't know. They've caught him with paint on his hands, but I figure if they can't find the rest of the stuff, they can't arrest him, although they still have him red-handed, so to speak."

"Is dumping or hiding the stuff illegal?" she asked.

"Probably. Will you do it?"

"Of course—I'm just confirming."

"And can you also gather all our stuff from here too and put it in my locker?"

I turned and left the classroom.

"I thought you were getting your things," one of the officers said.

"I got somebody else to do it."

"You might want to get somebody else to clear out his locker," he suggested. "We can't go in there without a warrant, and that won't be coming until after we question him—assuming we get information that would justify a search."

"My client—I mean, my friend has nothing to hide. Do you?"

Oswald shook his head.

"He's innocent."

"Lawyer's kid," the officer said.

Chapter Fourteen

We sat silently in Mr. Roberts' office. Why was it taking my mother so long? But really, what was she going to do? There was the evidence, right on Oswald's hands. I'd seen enough episodes of *CSI* to know the police could match the paint on his hands with the paint on the billboard even without the cans of spray paint or his clothing.

With or without my mother, with or without the evidence, he was caught red-handed.

"I was just wondering," I said. "Why did you come for the two of us?"

"The mayor suggested your names."

"But how would he know about us?"

"Apparently he had somebody checking out Facebook sites for students at your school and found out that you two had been involved in a couple of things—a protest against school uniforms and something about an Internet campaign against Frankie's Restaurants."

I shook my head. It was bad enough to be Internet-creeped by your mother, but by the mayor and his henchmen? That was *so* wrong.

There was a knock on the door. Before anybody could react, it opened and Julia walked in. What was she doing here?

"Hi, Mr. Roberts. Sorry—I didn't know you were with people. I just wanted to say hello." She held up her hand to wave. It was covered in paint! Somehow, in moving the pack, its contents had gotten all over her hand.

The officers saw it too and got to their feet.

"And there are some other people who just wanted to say hello," she said.

Julia opened the door wide. Standing there outside Mr. Roberts' door was a line of kids. And even from where I sat, I could see that they all had paint on their hands.

The officers walked out into the main office, and we followed. The line of students extended out of that office and into the hall. We walked farther out. The line went down the entire hall and disappeared around the corner. It wasn't just a few students or even one or two classes. It looked like it was all of them, and everybody had paint on one or two hands. Then I noticed it wasn't just the students, but some of the teachers too. Mr. Singh was standing there, his hands as red as his turban. And there was Mrs. Johnson, and two of the gym teachers, and what looked like all of the cafeteria ladies.

"How did you do this?" I hissed at Julia.

"I told them it was for Oswald, that he was in trouble, and everybody just volunteered. Do you know anybody who doesn't like Oswald?"

"Not a soul...except for maybe the mayor." I paused. "You, Julia, are amazing."

"Of course I am, and you two jerks should have told me what you were doing."

"In my defense, I just found out yesterday—or really, in the middle of the night. Wait...defense." I ran up to the two officers. "I'm not sure if I can get a lawyer for everybody, but I assume that if you're going to interview Oswald, you'll have to interview everybody."

The officer stared at me. Then he broke into a smile and started to laugh. Not what I'd expected.

Then I heard a bellow. It was Mayor Dumfrey. He must have heard what was happening and come out to see. He stormed up to the officers.

"Arrest them! Arrest them all!"

"You want us to arrest an entire school, including the staff?" the officer asked.

"Yes, all of them. They think they can make a fool of me!"

"I think you don't need any help with that," I said. "You do a pretty good job of that on your own."

The mayor's eyes bulged, and for a split second I thought he was going to take a swing at me.

"They're nothing but a bunch of *stupid* students, and you haven't heard the last of this!" he yelled. "None of you!"

I looked around. Many of the kids had their phones out, snapping pictures and taking videos of what was happening. The mayor was right in that last statement—I was pretty sure nobody had heard the last of this.

He turned and stomped away, trailed by his bodyguards. I couldn't help but notice that they both looked amused. A roar went up from the crowd, and the line of students broke and rushed around Oswald and me and Julia and the two officers.

Oswald tapped me on the shoulder and gestured to his mouth.

"Yes, of course you can talk now!"

"Does this mean I'm not being arrested?" he asked one of the officers.

"Arrested? Are you joking? I wouldn't be surprised if they built a statue of you."

Oswald burst into laughter, and then somebody started chanting, "Oswald, Oswald, Oswald," and then more and more kids were chanting, and then it was everybody, and it was deafening. Three guys from the football team picked Oswald up, hoisted him onto their shoulders and carried him through the crowd and down the hall.

"Look out for the door frame!" I screamed, but nobody could hear me, and his head clunked against it, almost knocking him off before they reclaimed their grip. He smiled and waved to the crowd.

"Good thing it was his head," Julia said.

"Good thing somebody was *using* their head. Your idea to get everybody involved was nothing short of brilliant. Don't you ever wonder why I love you so much?" I said.

"Love?" she asked.

"Well…you know."

"Actually, I do…or at least suspected."

Chapter Fifteen

"Turn it up," Oswald said. "I don't want to miss this."

I hit the remote and turned up the volume so we could hear the news.

"In a stunning turn of events, Mayor Dumfrey has been defeated at the polls," the newscaster said.

In the background was a picture of the mayor—the *former* mayor.

He looked like he'd eaten something very bad.

"Two weeks before the election, the polls showed that he had a commanding lead, which makes his landslide loss even more remarkable. Mayor Dumfrey, who through the power of YouTube is now known internationally as Mayor Humpty Dumfrey, was caught berating the students of a local high school. The video went viral, and over the last three days there have been over 1.1 million hits."

In the background, the video was playing.

"This all began with some street art depicting Mayor Dumfrey as Humpty Dumpty."

The background was now the mural.

"I'm glad they got a picture of that," Oswald said. "You know, for my portfolio. It's already been painted over."

"In the video that has caught fire, the mayor refers to the youth as 'a bunch of stupid students.' Throughout the city, almost overnight, a virtual flock of sheep has appeared. Hundreds of sheep have been painted, on walls, stores, billboards and signs, and with each sheep are the words *I'm not just a stupid sheep*, the word *sheep* crossed out and the word *student* written above it."

I couldn't help but laugh. Sheep were everywhere across the whole city, and Oswald hadn't painted a single one. They'd been created by people we didn't know—lots of them. People who knew they didn't have to be sheep.

Oswald took the remote and turned off the set.

"I'm going to miss that guy," he said.

"You are?"

He shrugged. "Where am I going to get my inspiration from now?"

"I'm sure you'll find something," Julia said. "Artists always do."

"So you admit that I'm an artist?"

"One of my favorites. Right up there with that Rembrandt guy."

"He's pretty good," Oswald said. "Did you hear that he was *abnormally* tall, a virtual *giant*?"

"At least eight feet tall is what I heard," Julia agreed.

"I wish he was here right now. Do you know what street art I could do if I had him to help me?"

"I have a feeling we're going to find out what you can do, even if you don't have him to help you," I said.

"I guess we'll have to wait and see," Oswald said. The expression on his face left little doubt that we *would* all see. He was an artist.

About Deadboy

Deadboy is an anonymous street artist whose work first appeared on the streets of Toronto in 2010 and became recognized for his humorous and critical depictions of Mayor Rob Ford, who famously declared "war on graffiti"once he was elected into office.

Working with stencils and posters, Deadboy (who studied visual arts and film) views street art as a way to bypass the snobbery of the "art world" and have direct communication with the public, as well as confronting the issue of just what "public space" is, when it's mostly saturated with corporate media and advertising.

"*I first met Eric Walters at my Solo Art exhibit in 2012. He told me that he was writing a new book about a kid who takes on a power-hungry mayor, using stencils and spray paint. By total fluke, the main character and I share many similarities. After reading* Tagged *I was amazed at how right he was.*

Tagged *captures the true essence of Street Art and the freedom and power it can bring to someone who has enough passion and drive to want to make a statement and bring a voice to the voiceless.*

I hope this book will inspire a whole new generation to pick up a spray can or paintbrush and show the world around them that imagination is limitless and important, and that one person can make a difference."

—Deadboy

For more information, visit
www.deadboyart.tumblr.com

Acknowledgments

I've been a fan of Banksy since I first became aware of his work. Some of those original pieces I was fortunate enough to see on the streets and walls of London. Then I saw the documentary *Exit Through The Gift Shop* and saw so much more. I was blown away but the sheer brilliance and daring of the work and the power of the political and social messages he was portraying. This book was inspired by Banksy, and others like him, who are not only taking back the streets but asking people to think—outside the box, outside the gallery and outside the boundaries. My thanks and admiration.

Eric Walters began writing in 1993 as a way to entice his grade five students into becoming more interested in reading and writing. Since then, Eric has published over seventy five novels and has won over eighty awards. Often his stories incorporate themes that reflect his background in education and social work and his commitment to humanitarian and social-justice issues. He is a tireless presenter, speaking to over seventy thousand students per year in schools across the country. Eric is a father of three and lives in Mississauga, Ontario, with his wife. For more information, visit www.ericwalters.net.

orca soundings

For more information on all the books in the Orca Soundings series, please visit **www.orcabook.com.**